315942

Falkirk Council

For Catherine Repman, with love. S.P.

For William. C.J.C.

OXFORD
UNIVERSITY PRESS

Great Clarendon Street, Oxford OX2 6DP

Oxford University Press is a department of the University of Oxford.
It furthers the University's objective of excellence in research, scholarship,
and education by publishing worldwide in

Oxford New York
Auckland Cape Town Dar es Salaam Hong Kong Karachi
Kuala Lumpur Madrid Melbourne Mexico City Nairobi
New Delhi Shanghai Taipei Toronto

With offices in
Argentina Austria Brazil Chile Czech Republic France Greece
Guatemala Hungary Italy Japan Poland Portugal Singapore
South Korea Switzerland Thailand Turkey Ukraine Vietnam

Oxford is a registered trade mark of Oxford University Press
in the UK and in certain other countries

British Library Cataloguing in Publication Data available

ISBN-13: 978 0 19 279192 4 (hardback)
ISBN-10: 0 19 279192 3 (hardback)

ISBN-13: 978 0 19 272545 5 (paperback)
ISBN-10: 0 19 272545 9 (paperback)

10 9 8 7 6 5 4 3 2

Printed in China

Little Lost Cowboy

Simon Puttock and Caroline Jayne Church

OXFORD
UNIVERSITY PRESS

Cowboy Coyote was lonesome
and lost, so he sat down and
howled at the moon up high.

'Arooo!

I'm lost and
I'm lonesome!'

The moon said, 'Cowboy, if you ask ME, you should follow the stars. They'll show you the way to go.'

Cowboy Coyote said, 'Thank you, Moon,' and looked up at the sky and followed the stars until . . .

OUCH! He bumped into a cactus.

Cowboy Coyote pulled the prickles from his nose and howled into the night.

'Arooo!

I'm lost and I'm lonesome and my nose is sore!'

A snake in the grass said,
'Cowboy, if you were to ask ME,
I'd say why don't you follow
your poor, sore nose?

Your nose will show you the way to go.'

So Cowboy Coyote said, 'Thank you, Snake,' and he followed his nose until . . .

Cowboy Coyote
wrung out his hat,

and dripped
in the night,
and howled,

'Arooo!
I'm lost and I'm lonesome
and my nose is sore
and I'm VERY wet!'

A bird in a bush said, 'Cowboy, if you were to ask ME, I'd say follow the river – it knows where it's going.'

So Cowboy Coyote said, 'Thank you, Bird,'
and he followed the river until . . .

EEEK!

He fell down a deep, dark hole.

Cowboy Coyote rubbed his poor,
bumped bottom, and howled in
the dark in the hole in the ground.

'Arooo!

I'm lost and I'm lonesome and
my nose is sore and I'm VERY wet
and NOW I've bumped my bottom!'

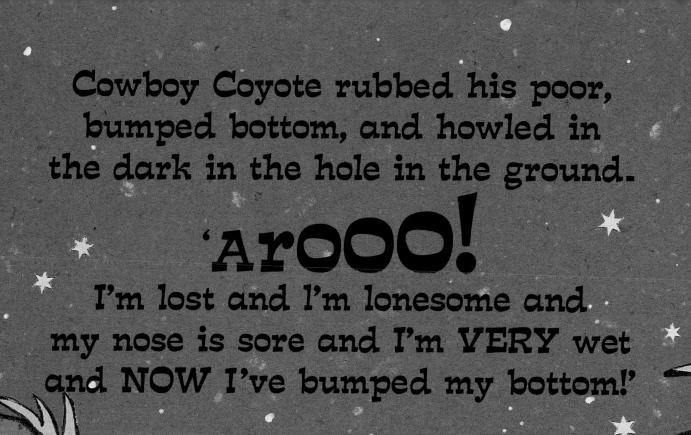

A toad in the hole said, 'Cowboy,
if you were to ask ME, I'd say
THIS is what to do –'

And Cowboy Coyote said,
'The moon said what to do
and I got a sore nose.

Snake said what to do
and I got VERY wet.

And Bird said what to do TOO
and I bumped my bottom.

So I'm not asking YOU. So there!"

The toad in the hole said nothing
at all. His feelings were hurt.
And Cowboy Coyote felt extra lonesome
and extra lost and a little bit mean as
well. So he did ask, after all,
'DO you know the way to get home?'

'Grrp,'

said the toad. 'No, I don't. But ...
if you sit tight and wait, and howl
your VERY LOUDEST,
I'm sure you will be found.'

So Cowboy Coyote sat tight
and waited, and howled his
VERY LOUDEST,

'Arooo!

I'm very lost and I'm ever so lonesome!
Except for dear, kind Toad!'

And a voice said, 'Cowboy,
what are you doing down THERE?'

'Oh, Mummy!' said Cowboy Coyote. 'I was SO lost and lonesome.

So I followed the stars and I bumped and I ouched ...

and I followed my nose and I tumbled and splashed.

Then I followed the river and fell down a hole....

THEN I stayed where I was and I howled and I howled. And YOU found me, Mummy!'

'Yes,' said Mummy Coyote. 'You made such a lovely ruckus – I just followed my ears. And my heart.'

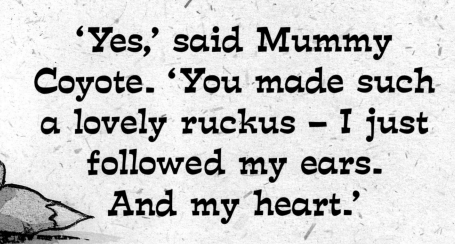

Then Mummy Coyote said, 'Cowboy Coyote, take hold of my tail and follow ME.'

So Cowboy Coyote held tight to his Mummy's tail and he followed her all the way home.

And they sang as they went
through the moonlit night,

'Arooo!

We're homeward and homesome!'